Butterfly Meadow

Three Cheers for Mallow!

Come flutter by
Butterfly
Meadow!

✤

Butterfly Meadow

Three Cheers for Mallow!

by Olivia Moss
illustrated by Helen Turner

SCHOLASTIC INC.

New York Toronto London Auckland Sydney
Mexico City New Delhi Hong Kong Buenos Aires

To Hannah Powell

With special thanks to Sue Mongredien

No part of this publication may be reproduced, stored in a retrieval system, or transmitted in any form or by any means, electronic, mechanical, photocopying, recording, or otherwise, without written permission of the publisher. For information regarding permission, write to Working Partners Limited, Stanley House, St. Chad's Place, London, WC1X 9HH, United Kingdom.

ISBN-13: 978-0-545-05458-4
ISBN-10: 0-545-05458-3

12 11 10 9 8 7 6 5 4 3 2   8 9 10 11 12 13/0

Printed in the U.S.A.

First printing, August 2008

Contents

CHAPTER ONE

Talent Search

". . . Eight, nine, ten! Ready or not, here I come!" called Dazzle. She was playing hide-and-seek with her best friend, Skipper, in Butterfly Meadow. Dazzle looked around, hoping to spot a flash of Skipper's blue wings. There was no sign of her friend. Where was Skipper hiding?

Dazzle fluttered through the air, searching the feathery grasses and colorful flowers. Ah! There was a splash of blue in the tall grass. Was it Skipper?

She dipped low for a closer look. No, it was a clump of bright cornflowers! Their blue heads were turned to the sun as they swayed in the gentle breeze.

Dazzle flew toward a patch of violet flowers. Maybe Skipper was hiding there. "I'm coming to find you!" she sang out, hoping her friend would giggle in reply.

Instead, a different butterfly's voice called out behind her. "All right, Team Butterfly! Let's G-O, go!"

Dazzle turned in surprise as a cloud of colorful butterflies swirled up from some nearby flowers, chattering and laughing. What was all the excitement about?

Skipper darted out from where she'd been hiding in the rambling rose. "Come on!" she cried.

"What's going on?" Dazzle asked, confused.

"Today is Sports Day," Skipper explained. "You know Mallow, the white butterfly over there. She's organizing it, just like she organized the party on your first day in Butterfly Meadow!"

Dazzle and Skipper joined the halo of butterflies hovering around Mallow.

"Quiet, please!" Mallow called.

She may be a small butterfly, but she's got a BIG voice, Dazzle thought, laughing to herself.

"Hi, everyone!" Mallow cried. "Today is our big Sports Day! We'll have the chance to compete against all the other creatures at Cowslip Pond."

"Will we have races, like last time?" asked Spot, a red-and-black butterfly.

"For sure," Mallow replied. "Speed races, obstacle races, backward flying races, you name it. And we've added a butterfly dance contest, too."

Skipper's wings quivered with excitement. "Can anyone take part?" she asked.

"Absolutely!" cried Mallow. "Everyone has a special talent. All you have to do is decide which event you want to try. Then we can fly to Cowslip Pond and start practicing!"

Dazzle could hardly keep still. The air filled with eager voices as all the butterflies began chattering.

"Wow! I can't wait!" a tiny green

butterfly shouted, bouncing on the breeze.

"I wonder who'll win the race this time," another butterfly said.

A white butterfly with black spots on its wings turned to Dazzle. "Which race are *you* going to enter?" it asked. "Long-distance? Short-sprint? Or maybe one of the obstacle races?"

Dazzle stopped short. "Um . . ." she replied. "I don't know."

"You don't know?" the spotted butterfly echoed.

Dazzle wasn't sure what to say. If everyone had a special talent, then she must have one, too. But she had no idea what it was!

CHAPTER TWO

Picking Teams

Dazzle glanced at Skipper, who was zipping back and forth between two tall plants. "What are you going to do at Sports Day?" Dazzle asked her friend.

"Race!" Skipper replied. "Maybe a short one, like the ten-lily-pad dash. How about you?"

Dazzle hesitated. Everyone else seemed so sure about what they wanted to do. "I don't know," she said.

Skipper touched the tip of her wing to Dazzle's. "Don't worry," she said kindly. "I'm sure you'll find something. It's like Mallow said — everyone has a special talent."

Skipper was right. There must be something she was good at! Then Dazzle remembered her first party in Butterfly Meadow, where she'd learned to dance. She felt a sudden rush of happiness. "Maybe I'll try the dance contest," she replied.

Twinkle, a beautiful peacock butterfly, whizzed by. A black-and-red-patterned butterfly flew right behind her. Twinkle skidded to a stop when she saw Skipper and Dazzle. The other butterfly had to swerve sharply to avoid bumping into her. "Hey!" he yelled.

Twinkle spun around. "Oh, sorry," she said, waving a wing. "Hi, there!" she cried to Dazzle and Skipper. "Have you met Stripe? He's a red admiral and is

very fast. Stripe, these are my best
friends — Dazzle and Skipper."

Stripe gave a little bow, bobbing
in the air. "Hi," he said. "Nice to
meet you."

"Hello," Dazzle
replied, looking at
his wings in
admiration. Stripe
had red bands
around the bottom
and top of his wings,
with white markings at the tips.

"Anyone want to race?" Stripe
asked, zipping up into the air. "Come
on, race me to the ash tree! Ready,
set, go!"

Before Dazzle knew it, Stripe had
flown off in a blur of red. Skipper

fluttered quickly after him. Dazzle
fluttered her wings, too, trying to catch
up. She flapped her wings as hard as she
could, but before she'd gotten very far,
she saw that Stripe had already looped
around the ash tree and was flying back.

"Whew!" Dazzle laughed as he
returned, with Skipper close behind.
"You *are* fast. I guess you'll be racing on
Sports Day?"

"You bet!" Stripe said with a grin.

Just then, Mallow appeared. "The
very butterflies I was looking for!" she
declared. "I've signed up for the relay
race. Now all I need are three other
butterflies for my team." She glanced
around. "Stripe, Twinkle, Skipper —
you're all fast fliers. Will you be on
my team?"

"Sure," Twinkle agreed at once. "I'm in!" Then she paused. "What *is* a relay race, anyway?"

"Each member of the team flies a part of the distance," Mallow explained. "When one racer reaches the next racer, he or she passes a petal. Once the petal has been given to the last butterfly, he or she heads to the finish line. First one over the line wins!"

"I've never tried the relay before,"
Stripe said. "It sounds like fun."

"I'd love to be on the team, too,"
Skipper said.

Dazzle felt her antennae droop. She'd
already decided to enter the dance
contest, but she couldn't help feeling
left out as the four butterflies huddled
for a team talk.

Skipper turned and gave Dazzle

an encouraging smile.
"You're going to enter
the dance contest, aren't
you, Dazzle?" she said.

"Yes, that's right."
Dazzle grinned and
showed Skipper her best
twirl.

"Cool," Mallow said. Then she flew
up high into the air. "Come on,
butterflies!" she called. "Let's fly to
Cowslip Pond!"

CHAPTER THREE

Dance Practice

Mallow led all the butterflies across the meadow and through the valley. Cowslip Pond was already buzzing when they arrived! Water striders twirled across the surface of the pond, practicing a complicated routine on their spindly legs. Dragonflies swerved back and forth through the reeds, their green-and-blue bodies shimmering. And striped bumblebees raced between the white, purple, and yellow irises, competing to collect the most pollen. "Keep going!" the bees' coach called from the sidelines. "Good job!"

"This is amazing!" Dazzle exclaimed, gazing around. She heard a chirping sound on the other side of the pond.

"That must be the Cowslip Pond Cricket Band," Skipper said, pointing a wing.

Dazzle could see a bunch of pale brown insects in the distance. They each had long legs and two pairs of wings. She remembered meeting crickets on her last trip to Cowslip Pond! They were all rubbing their front wings together at the same time to make the chirping sound.

"They're making music for the
dancers," Mallow added. "The dancers
are all meeting over on that side of the
pond, Dazzle."

Dazzle wriggled her wings. "I'd better
go join them," she said. "See you later!"

"Bye, Dazzle," Skipper said, waving
an antenna.

"Okay, team, it's time to practice,"
Twinkle said, turning to the others. "We
need to be the best at passing the petal.
A good petal-pass is the secret to
winning, you know. . . ."

Her voice faded as
Dazzle fluttered across
the pond. There, the
dancing butterflies had
organized themselves
into lines in the air. A

huge, amber-
colored monarch
butterfly was giving
instructions.

"And flap and turn and
dive to your right!" called the
monarch. She spotted Dazzle. "Are
you here to dance? Great! I'm
Tawny. Join in
whenever you're
ready!"

Dazzle joined a
line and tried to
follow Tawny's
instructions. She
had never done a routine like this before!

"Now loop-the-loop . . . one, two,
three, up!" Tawny chanted.

The air was full of color. More

butterflies than Dazzle could count spun all at once. She had never seen anything like it! She slowed down to watch a small turquoise butterfly do a perfect pirouette. But then Dazzle forgot to watch where she was going and . . .

Oh, no! Dazzle bumped into an orangey-red butterfly with pale blue spots along the edges of its wings. Their wings tangled together, and both butterflies swung through the air.

"That's an interesting new move!" Tawny laughed at the front of the group.

"Oops!" Dazzle giggled as the orangey-red butterfly untangled itself. "Sorry."

"Not a problem," the butterfly replied, smiling.

"Now left for three . . . and right for

three . . ." called Tawny. "Keep up in
the back!"

Was Tawny talking to her? Dazzle
tried hard to keep up as the other
butterflies all rose and fell together.

She flew up . . . just as the others all flew down!

"My name's Honey," the orangey-red butterfly whispered to Dazzle. "Don't worry, you'll get the hang of it soon."

"I'm Dazzle," Dazzle replied, bumping into the brown butterfly in front of her. "Oops!"

Trying to talk and dance at the same time was impossible! Dazzle concentrated on following Tawny's directions, but the harder she tried, the more mixed up she got.

"This way!" Honey called out helpfully as Tawny instructed the group to flutter in a circle. "Just follow me, Dazzle."

Dazzle was grateful that Honey was there to help her. Flying in a circle

sounded easy, but it was actually pretty tricky.

"Okay, let's take a break," Tawny said. The crickets fell silent. All the butterflies fluttered down to rest on the flowers at the side of the pond.

Dazzle and Honey were sipping nectar when Tawny flew up to them. "Dazzle, you'll make a wonderful backup flier for the dance contest," she said. "Thanks for all your hard work. I'll let you know if we need you for the competition."

"Oh," said Dazzle quietly. "Does that mean I didn't make the team?"

Tawny shook her head. "Not this time, dear. Sorry," she said.

CHAPTER FOUR

The Big Parade

Dazzle said good-bye to Honey and flew away, feeling disappointed. She decided to see what Skipper and the others were doing. Maybe it would cheer her up!

She found Skipper hovering in midair near the edge of the pond. "I'm waiting for Twinkle," Skipper explained. "We're

practicing our relay race. Oh, here she comes! I'd better get ready."

Twinkle was coming up fast behind Skipper, carrying a long white daisy petal. "Here!" she cried, passing the petal to Skipper.

Skipper took it, then streaked away like a bright blue line along the edge of the pond. "Go, Skipper!" Twinkle called after her. Then she turned to Dazzle. "Didn't my wings look magnificent as I flew? I must have been quite a sight."

Dazzle hid a smile. Twinkle was very proud of her large red wings. They had beautiful blue, purple, and pale yellow circles on them. "Oh, yes," Dazzle told her friend. "You were, Twinkle."

The two butterflies watched as
Skipper passed the petal to Stripe. He
flew the third stretch of the pond and
thrust the petal at Mallow. She fumbled
to get a hold of it, then set off on the last
leg of the race.

"We're still not fast enough," Twinkle
said, sighing. "Not as fast as them,
anyway." She pointed a wing.

Dazzle looked to see
another team of
butterflies whizzing
around the pond. "Who
are they?" she asked.

"Those are our rivals,"
Twinkle replied. "Spark, Buzz,
Sizzle, and Zing. They're *speedy*."

*Spark, Buzz, Sizzle, and Zing? Even
their names sound fast!* thought Dazzle. She

watched as the butterflies zoomed through the air. Their heads were down, their wings were flapping so fast you could barely see them, and they were passing a golden buttercup petal. Twinkle returned to her position for another practice race, and Dazzle wondered what to do next. It seemed like everyone had something to do at Sports Day — except her.

❋

"Good afternoon, Cowslip Pond!" a large brown toad croaked. "Sports Day is about to begin. All spectators, please take your seats to watch the opening ceremony!"

Dazzle was feeling
a little better now.
She had made
friends with Buddy,
a lacewing beetle. He
would not be taking part
in Sports Day either,
because he had a torn wing.
They sat together on a mossy log near
the pond to watch.

The parade started with the frogs.
They hopped around the wet grass,
croaking with
excitement. The
newts waddled
behind them,
their tails
swishing. Then
the insects sitting

near Dazzle and Buddy waved their
feelers and cheered. The bugs were up
next! Their hard shells shone in the sun.
Up above flew hundreds of butterflies,
a rainbow of colors against the blue
sky. Dazzle spotted her friends in the
group and waved her antennae at
them. "Skipper! Twinkle!" she called.
"Over here!" Skipper and Twinkle

grinned and fluttered their wings in her direction.

"Here come the dragonflies," said Buddy. "Aren't they awesome?"

Dazzle gazed at the beautiful dragonflies, skimming through the air at the end of the parade. Their wings shimmered with all the colors of the rainbow.

Finally, the queen bee flew gracefully through the air and came to a stop right above the center of Cowslip Pond. She looked around, her nose tipped up slightly in the air. Her golden stripes glowed in the sunlight.

"Let the games begin!" she declared.

CHAPTER FIVE

Watch Out!

Dazzle and Buddy watched the first few events eagerly. The frogs had a long-jump contest, then the grasshoppers competed in the high jump. A praying mantis was trying to find someone who would wrestle it, but nobody dared to go near its deadly jaws!

"It must be kidding," Buddy whispered to Dazzle. "Wrestle with the scariest creature at Cowslip Pond? No thanks!"

Next was the diving beetles' deep-dive contest in the pond. "Look," Buddy said, pointing a feeler toward the water. "See how the beetles tuck bubbles of air under

their wings? That's how they can breathe underwater."

"Cool," Dazzle said, impressed with everything her new friend was teaching her.

Next, it was time for the butterfly dance contest. Dazzle and Buddy fell silent as they watched the group of beautiful butterflies all dancing in perfect unison. Dazzle was happy to see that her friend Honey didn't make a single mistake. "I tried out for the dance routine," Dazzle told Buddy, "but I wasn't good enough."

"Don't worry," Buddy said. "I'm sure you're good at lots of other things."

Just then, Dazzle noticed how high the sun was in the sky. It was almost time for her friends' relay race! She decided to go

check up on them. "I'll be back soon," she told Buddy, fluttering off to the practice area.

As Dazzle flew up, she could hear Mallow hollering a special cheer.

"Mallow, Twinkle, Skipper, and Stripe;
We're the best racers, the fastest ones!"

Dazzle landed on a plant nearby. "That doesn't rhyme," Twinkle said to Mallow and Dazzle. "Aren't cheers supposed to rhyme?"

"How about 'the fastest type' instead of 'the fastest ones'?" Dazzle suggested. "That would make it rhyme."

"Good job, Dazzle!" Mallow said nodding her head and cheering again.

"Mallow, Skipper, Stripe, and Twinkle;
We're the best racers, the fastest type!"

"You got the names in the wrong

order!" Skipper giggled. "It still doesn't rhyme."

"Okay, okay," Stripe said, sighing. "We need to practice. The relay race is the big finale of Sports Day, and everyone will be watching. We've got to win!"

"He's right," Twinkle agreed. "Take your positions, butterflies!"

The four butterflies fluttered to their starting places. Twinkle flew first, passing the petal to Skipper. Skipper zoomed around to Stripe. Stripe took the petal and raced to Mallow. Finally, Mallow grabbed the petal and set off along the last part of the loop.

"Faster, Mallow, faster!" Stripe cheered.

Dazzle could see Mallow flap her

wings
even harder, trying to
speed up. But as she
rounded the final turn, a
dragonfly appeared from
out of nowhere.

CRASH!

Mallow flew right into the
dragonfly — and then
tumbled to the ground! She
didn't move. Was Mallow hurt?

CHAPTER SIX

Dazzle's Big Chance

Dazzle rushed over to her friend. "Mallow!" she cried. "Are you okay?"

Mallow seemed dazed. "My head is spinning," she said feebly.

Stripe flew over and checked Mallow's wings for rips or tears. "Nothing's broken," he said. "Can you fly?"

Mallow got up slowly, her wings trembling. She tried to fly but tumbled back to the ground again. "Sorry," she said quietly. "I feel a little shaky. I need to take a rest."

Skipper and Twinkle had arrived by now. "What's going on?" Skipper asked.

"I don't think I'll be able to fly in the race," Mallow told them sadly.

"Oh, no!" Twinkle cried.

"Do we have to drop out?" Stripe asked.

"Well, it's too late to find a new team member," Skipper said. "Unless . . ." She turned to Dazzle. "Unless *you* could take Mallow's place?"

Dazzle stared at her, surprised. "Me? But I'm not fast enough," she replied.

Twinkle, who was helping Mallow up, interrupted. "Oh, please say you'll do it!" she begged.

Stripe bent a flower over, so that Mallow could reach it and drink some nectar. "The team needs four racers," he said. "The race starts

soon, and we don't have time to find
anyone else."

"I don't know," Dazzle said
uncertainly. "You've practiced so hard! I
don't want to let you all down."

"You won't," Twinkle told her. "I
saw how fast you flew here when
Mallow got hurt. You're faster than you
think."

"And I can coach you," Mallow said,
between sips of nectar. "Please?"

Dazzle hesitated, then nodded.
"Okay. I'll try my best," she said.

Skipper, Twinkle, Stripe, and Mallow
all cheered. "That's the spirit!" said
Twinkle.

Stripe looked at Dazzle seriously.
"There's no time to lose."

"You'll be flying the last part of the race," Skipper said.

"And I'll be passing the petal to you," Stripe added, picking up the daisy petal. "Let's give it a try."

Dazzle and Stripe practiced. At first, Dazzle had trouble taking the petal and flying at the same time.

"Don't worry," Mallow said. "Once you get the hang of it, you'll be able to do it without thinking."

Mallow was right! It only took Dazzle a few more tries to learn what to do. Stripe flew up close to Dazzle's side. Then Dazzle started flying the minute she had taken the petal. She and Stripe tried the petal-pass again and again, faster and faster.

"That's good," said Mallow. "Remember to keep your antennae and body in a straight line, like an arrow, when you fly. And flap your wings in fast, small strokes."

"Got it," Dazzle said, practicing. *Fast and small, fast and small*, she murmured to herself as she sped along. The wind rushed past her. She never realized how

great it felt to fly fast! The speed made
her feel all giggly.

"Oh, and Dazzle?" called Mallow.
"The most important thing to remember
is to have fun! That's what today is all
about."

"I'll try," Dazzle said nervously. It
was strange how she felt scared and
excited all at the same time.

Just then, an announcement boomed
out across the pond. "Would all
butterflies competing in the team relay
race make their way to their starting
positions, please?"

"We're on!" Stripe cried. "Let's go,
guys. Time to show Spark and his team
a thing or two."

"Good luck, Dazzle," Mallow called,
flying carefully toward a spot where she

could sit and watch the race. "I'll cross my antennae for you."

"Thanks," Dazzle said, taking a deep breath. "I'll do my best."

I won't let my friends down, she vowed to herself as she flew. They had all been so nice, helping welcome her to Butterfly Meadow. Now it was Dazzle's turn to be a good friend to them!

CHAPTER SEVEN

Fast and Small

Dazzle and her teammates took their places around the pond with the three other relay teams. Three other butterflies lined up in the fourth position alongside Dazzle. Buzz, from Spark's team, was there.

Buzz cocked an antenna at Dazzle. "I've never seen you race before," he

said. "But if you're on Stripe's team, you must be good."

"I hope so," Dazzle replied. Her wings trembled. She hoped she could remember everything that Stripe and Mallow had taught her. If she was slow, they wouldn't win and she'd let her friends down. That would be awful!

One of the frogs let out a loud croak to signal the start of the race. And they were off! Four butterflies bolted into action and soared around the pond. Twinkle was one of them, flying as fast as her pretty wings would take her. Twinkle reached Skipper and passed her the petal. Skipper zoomed away, but made the mistake of looking behind her, which slowed her down. "Keep going, Skipper!" Dazzle called.

All of the spectators cheered for their favorite teams. "Fly, Zing, fly!" Dazzle heard some ladybugs yelling.

Skipper caught up with Zing, from Spark's team, and stayed next to him for their leg of the race. Then she passed the petal to Stripe, who bolted ahead. He flew clear of the whole pack!

The audience was getting really excited now. The frogs hopped up and down, croaking loudly. The newts stomped their feet. And the insects chirped, cheered, and shouted! "Go, Stripe! Go, Stripe!" a group of black-and-white butterflies chanted from the stands.

Stripe was getting closer to Dazzle, flying faster than she'd ever seen him fly before. Dazzle moved into position to grab the petal. Stripe seemed to be having trouble slowing down. *Maybe*

that's normal, Dazzle thought. But he was heading straight for her!

"Whoa," Stripe yelled . . . as he bumped right into Dazzle!

No one was hurt, but Stripe tumbled up ahead. Dazzle had to zoom forward to catch up with him and grab the petal. Meanwhile, Buzz had flown into the lead. Oh, no! Dazzle's team was losing. It was all up to her now. She *had* to get back in the race.

Fast and small, fast and small, Dazzle reminded herself as she flapped her

wings. But Buzz was still up in front of
her, his purple wings beating even faster.

Then, through the cheers of the
crowd, Dazzle heard a familiar voice:

"Dazzle, Twinkle, Skipper, and Stripe
You're the best racers, the fastest type!"

It was Mallow. She had changed her
cheer to include Dazzle's name!

Dazzle felt an extra burst of energy.

She flew even faster,
and pulled level with
Buzz. She could see the
finish line up ahead.
Come on, Dazzle! she
told herself. Her wings
were starting to feel tired,
but with one final push, she
bolted ahead of Buzz
at the last second. Her team had won!

CHAPTER EIGHT

The Real Reward

Dazzle felt dizzy with excitement. She could hardly believe it! Stripe, Twinkle, Mallow, and Skipper flew over to celebrate, tapping their wings together joyfully. The crowd cheered. Dazzle could see Buddy in the audience, clapping his antennae and beaming proudly.

"I knew you could do it," Skipper told Dazzle, grinning.

"Great job, Dazzle!" Mallow cried. "Seeing you race across that finish line made me feel a whole lot better."

"It was your cheer that helped me go faster," Dazzle told Mallow. "That was just what I needed!"

The queen bee hovered above the center of the pond again, and the crowd fell silent. "What a wonderful Sports Day," she said. "Everyone who's participated is a winner, but special congratulations go to those who won first place in their events."

The audience applauded as the queen bee circled the pond, handing out awards. As she approached Dazzle and her team, Dazzle was so excited she could hardly keep her wings still!

Dazzle glanced around and spotted Mallow watching from a nearby plant. "Mallow, come here," she called to the little white butterfly. "You're the one who put this team together in the first place. We wouldn't have won without you!"

Mallow flew over to join the team
as the queen bee came to a stop in
front of them. Mallow smiled at
Dazzle. "Thank you, Dazzle," she
whispered. "You did a lot to help our
team today."

The queen bee gave Dazzle, Skipper,
Twinkle, Stripe, and Mallow a touch of
golden pollen on their wings. "You all

did very well," she told them. "What an exciting race!"

Dazzle felt as if she might burst with pride. "Thank you," she managed to say, dipping her head respectfully.

"Oh, look how the pollen sparkles on my wings!" Twinkle cried as they all flew back to the sidelines. "They're even more beautiful than usual."

Dazzle smiled. She loved how the golden pollen shimmered on her yellow wings, too, but for her, the real reward had been racing with her friends and being part of a team. She would never forget that!

"Three cheers for Sports Day," Mallow called out. "Hip-hip . . ."

"HOORAY!" cried all the creatures around Cowslip Pond.

"Hip-hip . . ."

"HOORAY!"

"Hip-hip . . ."

"HOORAY!"

Dazzle twirled in the air, bursting with happiness. It had been a perfect day with her friends — one that she would never forget.

FUN FACTS!
More than Beautiful

When you think of butterflies, you picture their colorful wings. But butterfly wings are more than just beautiful!

Each butterfly family can be identified by the size, shape and color of its wings. Some butterflies have large and colorful wings, such as the peacock butterfly. Other butterflies, such as the pale clouded yellow, have wings of only one color. Butterfly wings are made up of millions of scales. These scales are so tiny that, to us, they look like nothing more than powder!

Butterflies use their wings to help them twist, turn, dive, and soar through the air. Some butterflies can fly as fast as twelve miles an hour! They can also travel great distances. The monarch butterfly has been known to fly across Mexico and the United States, a distance of more than two thousand miles.

Butterfly wings can also help butterflies hide or scare off predators — animals or insects that might eat them. Some butterfly wings are colored to look like their surroundings, so they can be hard to see. The bright colors on other butterfly wings warn predators to stay away, because this type of butterfly might taste bad or be poisonous. Some butterfly wings even have spots that look like eyes!

A butterfly needs wings to look pretty, fly fast, and stay safe. If you were a butterfly, what kind of wings would you have?

Dazzle is finally at home in

Butterfly Meadow!

Here's a sneak peek at her next
adventure,

Skipper to the
Rescue!

CHAPTER ONE

New Furry Friends

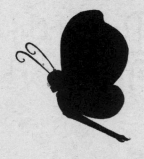

Whoooooosh! The long grasses of Butterfly Meadow swayed in the wind. "The breeze makes me want to fly high into the sky," Dazzle said to her friend Skipper, as the wind tugged at her small, yellow wings.

"Me, too," Skipper replied. "Let's go exploring!" She fluttered her blue wings and turned to Twinkle, a peacock butterfly, and Mallow, a small white butterfly, who were barely balancing on nearby flowers. "We're going flying. Want to come?"

"Sure," Mallow agreed.

Twinkle was busy admiring her colorful wings, but looked up at Skipper. "Sounds like fun," she said. "Lets go!"

The four friends took to the air, sailing along on the breeze. "Wheeeee!" Mallow cried as the wind carried them toward the forest.

Dazzle raced to catch up with her friends, and they reached the forest in no time.

Long, green sycamore seeds were falling from a nearby tree, twisting and turning as they floated to the ground. Dazzle's friends all started zipping in and out of them. Skipper was especially good at darting in between the seeds, swerving nimbly so she wouldn't get hit.

Dazzle joined in. "This is fun!" she cried, ducking and diving like her friends. "I love the way the seeds spin around and around. They look almost like butterflies' wings!"

"Those little wings help the seeds float from the tree," Twinkle explained. "They'll have a better chance of growing big and tall if they land away from the mother tree's roots.

Just then, a stronger gust of wind blew through the forest, and Dazzle had to dive away from the tree to avoid the shower of seeds. She quickly gazed around, floating in the air. Where had her friends gone?